The BOX

by Yvette Cragun

illustrated by Alex Smith

pink umbrella books

PHOENIX, ARIZONA

ISBN: **978-0692787410**

Published by Pink Umbrella Books (www.pinkumbrellapublishing.com)

Yvette Cragun, 1978- author.

 The Box / Yvette Cragun.

 A little boy uses his imagination to transform a cardboard box into many different adventures.

ISBN : **978-0692787410**

 Library of Congress Control Number: 2016956576

Illustrations by Alex Smith

Illustration © 2016 Alex Smith

Cover design by Adrienne Quintana

Cover design © 2016 Adrienne Quintana

For my boys

Look at this box. It's just lying about. Who in the world would have thrown this thing out?

It's amazing! It's awesome! It's great as can be! I think I will move it right under my tree.

I'll make it a fort where I stash all my things:

a bucket, some Legos, my baseball,

some strings.

It's looking so good. I'm feeling so proud. I hang up my sign that says *no girls allowed*.

Now all I need are some friends to come play. They'll think it's so great, we'll stay in it all day.

It turns into so many wonderful things.

A ship for us pirates.

A castle for kings.

An animal clinic where all the dogs bark.

A submarine that keeps us
all safe from the sharks.

A place for us cowboys to
hang up our hats.

A cave that is home to ten thousand bats.

A race car...

A dump truck...among
other things

It can take off and fly when
we make it have wings!

The parents have come to pick up their boys. They find us, no trouble, they just follow the noise.

Now I'm alone with the thoughts in my head. I wonder what would happen if I brought out my bed.

"This could be my new room!" I tell mom with a grin. I really am hoping she'll let me move in.

She doesn't see it. Oh how can she not? I know we're looking at it from the same spot.

As I sit on the porch with a heart full of sorrow, I have to remember there'll be more fun tomorrow.

CPSIA information can be obtained
at www.ICGtesting.com
Printed in the USA
LVHW02s0511170218
566965LV00006B/36/P